Daddy's Little Squirrel

Kayla Shurley Davidson

Illustrations by
Stephen Adams

AuthorHouse™
1663 Liberty Drive
Bloomington, IN 47403
www.authorhouse.com
Phone: 833-262-8899

Because of the dynamic nature of the Internet, any web addresses or links contained in this book may have changed
since publication and may no longer be valid. The views expressed in this work are solely those of the author and do not
necessarily reflect the views of the publisher, and the publisher hereby disclaims any responsibility for them.

Any people depicted in stock imagery provided by Getty Images are models,
and such images are being used for illustrative purposes only.
Certain stock imagery © Getty Images.

This book is printed on acid-free paper.

ISBN: 978-1-4490-8474-5 (sc)
ISBN: 978-1-4918-5096-1 (e)

Library of Congress Control Number: 2010914330

Print information available on the last page.

Published by AuthorHouse 09/30/2022

authorHOUSE®

In loving memory of my father,
Scott Thomason Shurley

There once was a girl named Kallie. Every day, Kallie would wake up her father by asking him, "Daddy, can I go to the ranch with you today?"

Her father would stretch, yawn, and then say, "I would be glad to have you come along. I could sure use the help."

As always, Kallie rushed to her closet, grabbed a pearl-snap work shirt, a pair of blue jeans, and boots, and began getting ready for the big day. Kallie and her father did all sorts of activities together. They would ride around the ranch, set up traps to catch bobcats, count and feed the cattle, and collect special rocks for Kallie to keep.

On really special days, they would also round up goats on their horses, Solo Freckle and Copland Scott. A day never passed that Kallie's father did not tell her how much he needed and loved her help.

In town, people would pass Kallie and her father on the street, often remarking how Kallie looked just like her daddy. Kallie's daddy would proudly tell them, "Yep, I've got my helper with me today." Kallie always glowed at the thought of being so important.

One night, while tucking Kallie in, her daddy said, "In the morning, remind me to go to the post office to check the mail."

Kallie touched her memory rock on her nightstand as she said, "Don't worry, Daddy. I would never forget."

"Goodnight, Little Squirrel. Sweet dreams," Kallie's daddy said, but she was already asleep.

The next day, Kallie and her daddy drank their coffee and milk, fed the horses, and checked the water troughs. As the two of them were pulling up to the post office, Kallie remembered her father's request. "Don't forget! We have to go to the post office," Kallie said.

"What a great helper you are, Squirrel. I had forgotten all about the post office," her father replied.

The next night, while tucking Kallie in, her daddy said, "In the morning, remind me that we have to go to the Llano pasture to feed the cows."

Kallie touched the memory rock on her nightstand as she said, "Don't worry, Daddy. I would never forget."

"Goodnight, Little Squirrel. Sweet dreams," Kallie's daddy said, but she was already asleep.

The next day, Kallie and her daddy drank their coffee and milk, fed the horses, and checked the water troughs. As they were driving into the Llano pasture, Kallie remembered her father's request. "Don't forget! We have to go feed the cows, Daddy," Kallie said.

"What a great helper you are, Squirrel. I had forgotten all about feeding the cows," her dad replied.

The next night, while tucking Kallie in, her daddy said, "In the morning, remind me that we have to call Grandmother to let her know what time we're picking her up for church."

Kallie touched the memory rock on her nightstand as she said, "Don't worry, Daddy. I would never forget."

"Goodnight, Little Squirrel. Sweet dreams," Kallie's daddy said, but she was already asleep.

The next day, Kallie and her daddy ran several errands. As Kallie's daddy was dialing the number to her grandmother's house, she remembered her father's request. "Don't forget! We have to call Grandmother," Kallie said.

"What a great helper you are, Squirrel. I had forgotten all about calling Grandmother," her daddy replied.

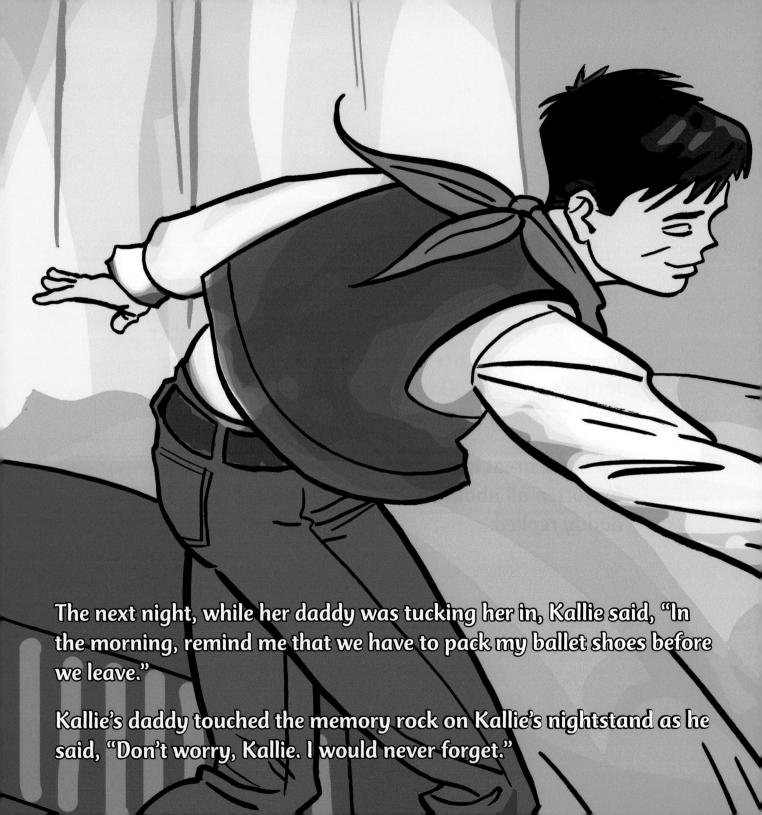

The next night, while her daddy was tucking her in, Kallie said, "In the morning, remind me that we have to pack my ballet shoes before we leave."

Kallie's daddy touched the memory rock on Kallie's nightstand as he said, "Don't worry, Kallie. I would never forget."

He finished tucking her in and said, "Goodnight, Little Squirrel. Sweet dreams." But she was already asleep.

The next morning after breakfast, as Kallie was putting her ballet slippers in her bag, Kallie's father remembered her request. "Little Squirrel, don't forget to pack your ballet shoes," Kallie's father said.

"What a great helper you are, Daddy," Kallie replied. "I had forgotten all about my ballet shoes."

Printed in the United States
by Baker & Taylor Publisher Services